I0726939

Stories of the Veil

ASTRA

ASTRA

THE UNVEILED

PEPPER MCGRAW

P
M
G
Publishing

CONTENTS

CHAPTER 1

MORTAL SIDE OF THE WESTERN VEIL, LAWRENCE, KANSAS

*K*ahji Nenzele kept his back to the Veil and his eyes on the chaos of the battle around them.

The Veil hid Faerie from mortal eyes, but it was the shield Princess Astra had constructed around the Fae that concealed them.

Despite the shield, as Captain of the Royal Guard, Kahji didn't trust that things wouldn't go wrong in a heartbeat, especially when the college campus he'd expected was instead a battlefield overrun by mortals attacking one another.

The only good news was that none of the mortals appeared to be carrying swords.

Instead, they used their bodies as weapons, hurtling themselves at each other, hitting the ground and piling on top of one another before standing and beginning the process again.

It was the weirdest battle Kahji had ever seen. It seemed to move back and forth across the field in some strange pattern he couldn't quite discern.

In addition to the warriors on the field, Kahji also had to worry about the thousands of shouting mortals seated in tall structures on all four sides of them.

Kahji had a flash of memory from the far distant past: mortal gladiators, a giant colosseum, screaming spectators. It seemed the mortals had not changed much since the last time he had visited their realm.

At that moment, the mortal warriors all turned and barreled down the field toward them.

Kahji settled his hand on the hilt of his sword, ready to draw it should any of them manage to breach the shield Astra had constructed.

When they reached it, though, the runners blipped from one side to the other and continued running, seemingly unaware they had skipped an entire section of the field.

"Something's wrong," Astra exclaimed. "It's not working."

"What's not working?" Kahji winced as multiple warriors launched their bodies at another and they all went down in a pile of limbs.

"The Veil. It should have strengthened by now. It's

getting worse."

Kahji's attention snapped back to the Veil.

She was right.

The fractures in the Veil were spreading, rather than closing as usual. "Perhaps the Guardians haven't sealed themselves to it yet."

"No. They *have*. Something's wrong."

As if in response to her statement, the ground trembled beneath them and a white light exploded from the Veil, lighting up the field and sending all the warriors there, both Fae and mortal, to the ground.

Kahji woke to a silence that blanketed the world.

He struggled to his knees and crawled to Princess Astra's side.

Her eyes snapped open. "It's down," she whispered.

"What is?"

"The Veil."

For the second time that day, Kahji's attention snapped to the Veil, or at least to where it should have been.

The doorway to Faerie was still there, but this time, there was no Veil shielding Faerie from mortal eyes.

Kahji leapt to his feet, then reached down and pulled Astra to hers.

A quick glance around them revealed that Astra's shield was down as well.

This was not good.

The doorway to Faerie was clearly exposed, providing *thousands* of mortals, both warriors on the field and spectators in the seats above, a view of Faerie few of their kind had ever seen.

Worse yet, the Fae's glamour had fallen, unveiling their true forms to the mortals.

Astra fairly glowed with the magic of Faerie, causing the mortals to fall silent at the sight of her.

"I can't access my magic, Kahji," Astra muttered.

"I know. I can't either."

"Without our glamour, we're completely exposed out here."

A man dressed in a black and white shirt, shoved to the front of the mortal warriors and stormed toward Kahji and Astra, shouting, "What do you think you're doing, interrupting the game like that? Get off the field!"

"We can't do that, Kahji, not with Faerie exposed like this."

"Guardians!" Kahji shouted. "Defend the Princess and guard the entrance to Faerie!"

The Royal Guard scrambled into position. Four Guardians surrounded the doorway to Faerie while Dyranel and Zanzor joined Kahji at Astra's side.

All seven of the Royal Guard drew their swords and pointed them at the mortals.

Kahji nudged the princess backward toward the Veil

and snapped at the mortals advancing on them, "Stand back."

Astra ignored Kahji and called to the mortals, "You need to stop," then muttered to Kahji, "They aren't armed. Don't do anything rash."

"Armed or not, they're still warriors and there are too many of them at that. The seven of us cannot possibly hold back the tide. You need to return to Faerie at once."

At that moment, an entire unit of Fae Guardians poured in from Faerie. Three of them joined Astra and Kahji and the rest spread out in a protective circle around the doorway.

"We cannot leave the entrance to Faerie unprotected this side of the Veil," Astra said. "And I'm not leaving a single Fae behind, especially when our glamour has failed and we can't seem to tap into the magic of Faerie."

"Astra." Exasperation filled Kahji's voice. "Things are going to get ugly fast."

"I'm *not* leaving."

The sound of sirens filled the air and a few moments later, mortals Astra recognized as their version of Guardians stormed across the field toward them.

She was afraid Kahji was right. Things were about to get ugly.

Then it happened.

The Veil came up with an almost-audible pop. For one second, Astra couldn't breathe as the Veil drew energy from every Fae present to form anew.

A quick glance at the mortals, then back to the Veil, and Astra knew it was still not shielding Faerie from mortal eyes. Instead—she brushed up against the Veil with her magic and instantly understood that none of them would be going home anytime soon.

The Veil had solidified into a transparent shield that protected Faerie from anyone crossing into its lands, including the Fae now locked in the mortal realm.

The only good news was that with the Veil's return, Astra now had access to the magic of Faerie and her own power once more.

The mortal Guardian force, who had faltered at the sight of the many Fae with swords drawn and once more at the sight of the doorway to Faerie, recovered and surged forward.

"Put down your weapons," a mortal Guardian shouted even as his entire force pointed *their* weapons at the Fae.

Astra sighed.

Really.

Could nothing be simple anymore?

Kahji let out a growl of true anger and stepped in front of her, shielding her from the mortals' weapons.

That simple movement set off a chain reaction of events.

A popping sound filled the air and Kahji let out a grunt as he was flung backward into Astra.

They both fell to the ground as more pops sounded and a mortal shouted, "Hold your fire. Hold your fire!"

As the Fae realized they were under attack, they moved swiftly to surround their wounded and began wielding their swords as shields, pinging tiny pieces of metal back toward the mortals who were attacking them.

"Enough!" Astra shoved her magic outward in a huge surge of power.

Lightning rippled across the field, freezing mortals and Fae alike.

She struggled from beneath Kahji and saw that blood was pouring outward from where he'd fallen in a spreading lake of Fae power.

She let out a scream of pure rage and flung her power into that lake, lifting each tiny droplet of blood upward.

Her power caught Kahji in its grip and brought him back to standing.

The droplets of blood flowed back into the multiple wounds in his shoulder, chest and thigh.

The bullets that had exited his flesh ripped free from the ground and a wooden post twenty feet behind where Kahji and Astra had been standing and traveled their pathway backwards, sliding through Kahji's form, flesh and bone knitting behind them, as they returned to the weapons from which they had been fired.

As Astra's power wrapped around Kahji's form, he was lifted higher into the air, the bright light of her magic lighting up his form.

The sight of him still unconscious fueled Astra's fury. The lighting whip of her power whirled around the field in ever-increasing surges, intensified by rage and pain and fear.

That power yanked mortal weapons from the hands of the men and women who held them, crushing those weapons to dust in seconds.

"We are the Fae," she roared as she stormed away from where Kahji still hovered mid-air, his form still blanketed in the healing waves of her power.

Those waves spread ever outward, first covering the other Fae who had been felled by those same pieces of metal that had wounded Kahji, then covering those mortals who had fallen when the Fae had deflected their weapons back toward them.

"We are the Fae," she repeated, her voice echoing

across the field and into the stands where many mortals still sat, frozen in silence as they watched the confrontation on the field below. "We do not yield to mortals. We do not fall at your feet just because you wish it to be so. We are the immortal Fae and as is our right, by virtue of the Fae blood spilt upon these lands, we now claim them for the Fae."

She used her power to lift every mortal on the field, wounded and not, and began to move them farther and farther away from her fallen Fae warriors.

Her power stretched outward, sweeping up the mortals in the stands all around her, carrying them out of the stadium in every direction and leaving them, frozen and silent on its perimeter.

As the stands emptied of mortals, she sent another contraction of her power whipping through, lightning-fast, compressing and disintegrating the entire structure in seconds.

Her power then whipped across the field, disintegrating everything unnatural in its path. Boards, signs, lampposts, flashing lights, everything that wasn't part of the living earth compressed into dust.

She stopped in the center of the field and turned in a circle, eyeing the mortals she had dropped at the edges of where their stadium had once stood.

She settled the mortal Guardians and the warriors who had been playing their game on the field just outside where the stadium's screen had once stood, on the far opposite end from where her warriors recovered from their wounds.

She glared at the mortal warriors, fury still a bright burn in her blood.

The mortals stood silent in every direction, all of them still wrapped in her power, frozen in stillness and silenced by it.

She let the moments stretch, one after the other, giving the mortals time to reflect on their powerlessness in the grip of the Fae, before finally pulling her power back.

As it slowly contracted away from the mortals, she shaped it into a giant shield that snapped into position where the stands had once stood, forming a barrier around land the Fae would never again yield to the mortals.

When the shield settled into place, she rose into the air and glared down at the mortal Guardians who were still frozen and silent, though they had been released from her power. "We have shown you mercy. The power of Faerie has healed every mortal injured by the foolishness of your own Guardian force. Do not make the mistake of believing we will show you that same mercy again, for I assure you, we will not. Go home now. This land we have claimed for the Fae."

Astra.

*K*ahji's entire form was engulfed in heat. He could feel her essence burning through every fiber of his being, prying open that pathway he'd sealed off eleven hundred years before.

He came back to the world fully erect, on fire for the Fae he had loved throughout eternity.

Astra.

She hovered high above the field that still crackled in the wake of her fire.

White lightning zipped across the field and up into the sky, traveling a path in reverse, surging from the land beneath them, wrapping everything he could see in its embrace.

He shuddered in the grip of an endless, burning need as she turned to face him, her gorgeous blue eyes shining bright in the falling twilight.

Astra.

Kahji?

The stunned wonder in her voice brought him back to his senses.

He shut down the pathway with a flick of his magic, acting out of both instinct and habit.

He struggled to tamp down his raging desire, to

prepare for the monumental effort of pretending these last few magical moments had never happened.

Having heard her voice in his head, something he'd never thought a possibility—having felt her magic in his blood and his veins, stroking across his skin—he wasn't certain he would succeed in that endeavor.

Indeed, it was quite possible he would go mad with the effort of continuing to deny their bond.

Still. He had to try.

Princess Astra was not for the likes of him.

The minute she heard his voice, Astra lost all interest in the foolish mortals.

She was turning toward him when she heard his voice again.

Astra.

With a sense of wonder and anticipation, she responded, *Kahji?*

No response.

He was where she'd left him, hovering mid-air on the other side of the field, far from where she'd taken the mortals. His eyes were on her, though, and she thought, even from this distance, that the way he looked at her in that moment was entirely new.

Then, his eyes shuttered and he was back to the Fae she knew: Captain of the Royal Guard and Royal Pain in her Arse.

"Astra," he shouted. "Get back here right now and let me down from here!"

She rolled her eyes, settled back on the ground and allowed the rest of her power, the lightning that still whipped across the field in increasingly smaller waves, to dissipate.

She strolled calmly toward Kahji as her power deposited him back on his feet and he surged toward her, the rest of the Royal Guard rushing in his wake.

Overprotective as usual.

The Guard surrounded her and Kahji launched into one of his favorite pastimes: lecturing her.

Most of it she had heard many times before, though there was the occasional new twist.

"You know you are not to leave the Guard's presence when we are traveling."

Never mind that the entire Guard had either been down or under attack.

"A princess does not ever show such a blatant overuse of power."

Never mind that her "blatant overuse of power" had ended the confrontation and healed the wounded.

"I cannot believe you would place yourself at such

risk, revealing your power to the mortals and exposing the Fae."

Now *that* she took extreme exception to. "Excuse me! I did *not* expose the Fae. The Veils fell and I assure you, I had nothing to do with that."

"Yes." Kahji glowered across the field at the unit of Guardians who stood near the Veil, prepared as always to defend it. "I know *exactly* who is responsible for that." He took off toward the Guardians of the Veil.

Astra hurried after him, worried that he might actually harm the Guardians they now needed more than ever.

"Explain to me exactly how this happened," Kahji shouted.

Kalina Wyendeh stepped forward, her mate, Thorne Evaria at her side.

"How could you fail in your one sacred duty to the Fae?" Kahji demanded.

"We have no idea what happened," Kalina said.

"We followed all of the rituals exactly," Thorne said.

Another Guardian of the Veil—Astra thought his name was Mitaru—stepped forward. "We did have two Guardians fall five weeks before the ceremonies. They were replaced by someone from the Reserves and by Thorne, who is an experienced Guardian from the East."

"I'm aware," Astra spoke quickly before Kahji could

start yelling again. "I do not believe such minor changes could possibly have had this impact." She eyed Kalina and Thorne. "Perhaps, though, a mated pair made all the difference."

Kalina blanched. "You think our mating caused this?"

"That was not our intent," Thorne said, a stricken look on his face.

"Your mating was blessed by the Fae Queen herself," Astra said. "This was not anticipated by any of us. The seers insisted Thorne needed to be at the Western Veil and that resulted in your mating. Given those facts, I cannot see how this could be anything other than the guiding hand of fate.

"But none of this matters right now. Not when we are locked in the mortal world, unable to return to Faerie, unveiled to mortal eyes."

"Our glamour is back," Kalina said. "We should be able to veil ourselves again, at least. Right?"

"Unfortunately, Fae glamour does not work on mortal eyes that have seen and accepted the truth," Kahji said.

"Then we should wipe their memories," Thorne said.

"It is too late for that," Astra said. "There were recording devices everywhere. We are well and truly unveiled."

CHAPTER 2

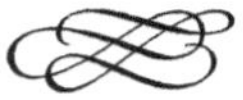

Four weeks in the mortal realm. *Four weeks.*

It was more than enough time to make any Fae go mad.

This was what Kahji kept thinking as he watched Princess Astra storm around the room, throwing things at him and shouting.

He'd gone mad.

It was the only explanation.

Centuries he'd kept this secret from her.

Not even once tempted to tell her the truth.

Well, maybe once.

Or twice.

A day.

But never had he actually done it!

Yet trap him for four weeks in the mortal realm and

apparently he went mad, blurting out the truth just because she asked for it.

Madness.

The rest of the Guard had all abandoned him to his fate.

Something he would have claimed was impossible.

If anyone had asked, he would have said the Guard he served with would never abandon him on the field of battle.

He would have been wrong though.

They couldn't flee fast enough.

The cowards.

He might have laughed at the looks on their faces when they realized what he'd admitted, but he'd been entirely too busy worrying about Astra's response to the news.

"I cannot believe you!" Astra shrieked.

Kahji sighed. This wasn't the first time she'd said this.

He stepped to the side and winced at the sound of the vase she'd hurled at his head breaking against the wall behind him.

He was actually quite relieved she was finally yelling. When he'd first admitted the truth, that they were mates and he'd known for centuries, she'd gone deadly silent.

The type of silence that usually signaled an impending death.

As he'd been sure it was his death she'd been plotting, he'd been quite relieved when an hour into the seething silence, she'd exploded into motion and starting throwing things and shouting at him.

By the fates, she was terrifying.

It took all his discipline as a Fae warrior not to claim her right then.

*A*stra could barely think.

She'd had a crush on the captain of her Royal Guard for as long as she could remember.

Centuries she'd wanted him.

But the pathway between mates hadn't opened when they'd met for the first time. She hadn't worried then, for she'd been under the age of majority.

She'd waited, longing for her hundredth birthday, absolutely certain that the moment they saw each other on that day, the path would open and they would claim each other as mates.

When her birthday came and went and nothing changed, she'd been devastated.

Until that moment, she'd worshipped Kahji,

following wherever he led, complying with his every demand, adoring him as only a child could.

When she'd realized the man she adored wasn't her fated mate, she'd spiraled downward. It had taken her another hundred years to recover her joy, to finally accept that some other Fae, not Kahji, was her destined mate.

She'd thrown herself into the search, dragging her Royal Guard all over Faerie, meeting as many Fae as she could, flirting with them all, driving Kahji mad, guarding her heart and pretending he wasn't still the love of her life.

And now, *eleven hundred years* past her majority, he was finally admitting they were mates?

It made no sense. He should *never* have been able to shield that truth from her.

Her rage waned as her brain kicked in and she began to think once more.

Of course, that didn't stop her from using her magic to launch yet another book at his egotistical, arrogant, *lying* head.

"Astra. Love. Let me explain."

"*Explain?* As if there could be any explanation for this."

"You were young when we met."

"Not that young! I was seventy-six years old, you pompous ass!"

"Entirely too young to become mate to someone approaching his two thousandth birthday."

This *again*. Always this. Like two thousand years made him ancient when those years were merely a drop in the vast oceanic lifespan of a Fae. "And what's your excuse for the *last* thousand years?"

"Even when you reached your majority, you were still so young. You hadn't had the opportunity to discover who you were. You looked at me with stars in your eyes."

Astra could feel herself blushing. "Well, don't worry. There aren't any stars anymore." She glared at him.

Kahji nodded. "That's good. You needed time to grow up."

"A thousand years?" she demanded dryly. "How did you manage it anyway?"

He sighed. "When mates meet and one is over the age of majority and the other is not, it's tradition for the one who is older to use magic to hold their pathway closed to keep the younger one's development from being influenced by the older one. You know this."

"Of course I do and I support that. Children have the right to grow into adulthood as individuals before being dragged into a mating. That doesn't mean you get to keep the pathway closed forever! I expected you to open it when I hit my majority. That you didn't—I thought that meant we weren't mates. You broke my heart, Kahji."

*A*t least she was finally talking to him, but hearing the pain in her voice, seeing the tears shining in her eyes, he wasn't sure she would ever forgive him.

By the fates, he'd made a mess of things.

He struggled for the right words, to somehow help her understand without hurting her worse than he already had. "I'm sorry, Astra, but you weren't ready. You would never have become the woman you are today—the strong princess, the potential Queen—if I had claimed you back then. You needed time to grow into your sense of self, into your *power*."

"As the mortals would say, *what a load of crock*. I might accept that answer if you'd only kept this from me for the first hundred years. Maybe even two hundred years. But for *eleven hundred* years, Kahji? Even I couldn't possibly take that long to mature."

"That's not what I meant, Astra, and you know it. I should have told you long ago, but the truth is allowing you the time to become who you were meant to be was a double-edged sword. You're amazing, Astra, in every way, and the more time that passed, the more I realized how unworthy of you I truly am."

For a second, Astra just stared at him, apparently speechless, then she shrieked, "Unworthy? You're the Captain of my Guard, for fate's sake! You've risked your life countless times, most recently taking mortal bullets to protect me. How could you possibly think you're unworthy?"

Before Kahji could reply, a throat clearing caught their attention. "Ah, Kahji, Astra, sorry to interrupt."

"What is it, Andri?" Kahji asked.

"The mortals are back. They claim to have papers that give them the right to force us off this land."

"Seriously?" Astra demanded. "I just can't even. These mortals are the bane of my existence. Stubborn, idiotic, self-righteous, hypocritical *thieves*! Do they think we do not know their history of land-snatching? Ugh. I am so done with this conversation."

Kahji just shook his head. "I told you they weren't going to accept, no matter how many times you eject them. They want these lands and they're not giving them up."

"I shouldn't have stopped at Mississippi Street. It just gave them ideas, like I wasn't serious when I said I would burn the rest of their territories to the ground if they kept coming back." She stormed past Andri and out the front door, tossing over her shoulder, "And don't think for a minute this conversation is over, Kahji. We're just getting started!"

"**W**as that really necessary?" Kahji demanded two hours later as he followed Astra back into her rooms.

Astra rolled her eyes, not at all surprised at his response. "Perhaps not, but I'm done trying to negotiate with these mortals."

"I'm sorry. I must have misunderstood. Are you saying that was a *negotiation?*"

"Of *course* it was a negotiation! I told them we weren't giving back the lands and they refused to listen, so I *made* them listen."

"Huh. It appears our definitions of *negotiate* are quite different."

"As the mortals would say, *whatever*. Now let's get back to this whole mate conversation. Explain to me again exactly *why* I had to wait more than *one thousand years* to find out you're my *mate!*" Astra was shrieking by the end, but she just couldn't help it.

The entire time she'd been with the mortals, *negotiating*, she'd been stewing over her memories of a thousand years of believing Kahji wasn't her mate: how brokenhearted she'd been in the beginning, the years she'd wasted searching for a mate she'd already met, the unsatiated hunger she'd felt whenever in his presence and how she'd struggled to tamp it down year after year after year.

A thousand years of agony and for what? So that he could claim he wasn't good enough for her?

It was completely outrageous, insufferable, maddening and absolutely *infuriating*.

"Astra. You could easily ascend to Queen one day."

"Bite your tongue! You know that Zivek will be King one day, which means his mate shall be queen."

"Unless something happens to him or he chooses not to ascend."

"Should that happen, one of my other brothers would ascend instead, and their mate would be queen." Thank goodness. Astra regularly gave thanks to the fates that they had seen fit to provide her with three older brothers who would take on the realm if need be. "I have no desire to be queen and you know it."

"I'm just saying it could happen, and Astra, whether you think so or not, you would make an excellent queen."

"Aw, that's sweet." Astra gave him her most insincere smile, then snarled, "But it still doesn't explain why we didn't mate *eleven hundred years ago!*"

"I'm a Guardian, Astra. It's what I do. I serve

Faerie and her Royal families. I fight when I need to fight and I will die if need be to protect those under my care. I am not meant to be king of the realm."

"And I'm not meant to be queen. I'm pretty sure we just established that. But if, in some nightmare alternate realm, I had to ascend, I would do so for the good of Faerie, and *so would you.*

"You just said it yourself, Kahji. You will fight and die to protect Faerie and all those under your care. Well, we Fae have a long history of Warrior Kings and Queens serving, then dying for Faerie. You and I, we would be no different." She glared at him, not certain what else to say to convince him, not even certain she *wanted* to convince him.

Why was she even trying? He clearly didn't want her. "Forget it. Obviously, you're not interested and that's fine."

"What? No. Astra—"

"It's fine." It infuriated Astra to hear the slight tremble in her voice. "I have to go. We'll talk more later."

"Astra —"

She ignored him and walked out.

He'd never lied to her before, but he was one of the most respected Guardians of the realm. How could he believe he wasn't worthy?

And did she want to try and convince him otherwise?

It had taken her weeks to come up with the courage to ask Kahji outright if he was hers.

In eleven hundred years, it had never occurred to her to ask because it had never occurred to her that he would willfully deprive them both of their destined mate. Then she'd heard his voice inside her head the day the Veils fell, and everything had changed.

She'd initially planned to ask him immediately, but they were so busy in the beginning, trying to figure out how to survive in this mortal realm, that she'd decided to wait until things calmed down a bit.

Once they had, it had still taken her days to figure out exactly what she wanted to say, then still more days to gather her courage to ask something no Fae should ever have to.

Because they should just *know*.

After eleven hundred years of believing they weren't mates, Astra knew that regardless of whether the answer was yes or no, she would always feel foolish for having asked the question.

And so, that morning, feeling a nauseating mix of hope and shame, she'd blurted out, "Kahji, tell me the truth. Are we mates?"

She hadn't even waited until they were alone. She'd wanted to be able to quiz the other Guardians if he denied it. She'd wanted witnesses who could tell her whether they thought he was speaking the truth or not.

He'd frozen in such a way, though, that she'd known, witnesses or no, he *was* her mate.

He'd looked at her with that look in his eyes, the one she'd seen on the field that day, filled with a blazing heat and a desire that had threatened to send her entire body up in flames.

Then he'd blinked and that Fae was gone, replaced by the typical, aloof, judgmental, *bossy* Captain of her Royal Guard and she'd just *known* he was going to lie.

"Don't lie," she'd snapped at him. "Tell me the truth, Kahji. *Are we mates?*"

He'd dragged in a deep breath and said, so softly she almost didn't hear the words, "We are."

The rest of the Fae had frozen the moment she'd asked the question and for one long moment after he'd answered, they'd remained frozen, as did she, then they'd all bolted for the door.

She'd simply stared at Kahji, ignoring the other Fae, lost in her memories of heartbreak and devastating loneliness.

She'd seethed, vibrating in fury, then eventually had exploded with it.

He hadn't tried to defend himself, though he had tried to explain, but she hadn't listened because eleven hundred years of memories were a roar in her ears that drowned out everything else.

She should probably let him explain again and this time really listen to the words, to the emotions beneath them.

But not yet.

Not today.

After all, she had suffered for eleven hundred years, believing he wasn't her mate.

He could definitely endure her wrath a bit longer.

CHAPTER 3

"It was a mistake to send away half the Guardians of the Veil." Kahji paced from one side of the courtyard to the other, flowers and blades of grass straining away from his boots as he passed.

Astra ignored him, focused instead on the tiny, iridescent hummingbird that had come to rest on her finger. So beautiful, so fragile, so extraordinarily fast.

The hummingbird took off, zipping to a flower, its movements almost too quick for even a Fae's eye to catch.

"Come on, Astra," Kahji said, exasperation clear in his tone. "You can't ignore me forever."

Actually, she could.

Besides, she was tired of this argument.

Not that they'd actually argued.

More like Kahji had yelled and lectured and paced and Astra had ignored him.

When he'd finally run out of energy and things to say, she'd turned to Kalina and ordered her to take half her unit to the east.

Basically, Astra had done something she rarely did: she'd pulled rank.

And enjoyed it.

Kahji had stewed and glowered as Kalina had gathered her unit and identified who would go with her and who would stay.

Of course, she'd immediately identified her best friend, Mitaru, and her mate, Thorne, as two who would accompany her.

Something that Kahji had also had much to say about.

He'd ranted that at least one of the three should remain with Astra, but both Astra and Kalina had overridden him, which had just made him angrier.

Kalina had ridden out with half her unit, just an hour before, and Kahji had been growling about it ever since.

"They even took all the horses. It took Rashideh and Lumina weeks to acquire those mortal beasts and now we have no means of transportation yet again."

Like the Guardians hadn't enjoyed using their magic

to travel all over the midwest, tracking down the fastest and strongest steeds available.

Like they wouldn't enjoy doing it again.

"Astra, come on. We can't go on like this. I'm the Captain of your Guard." Damn him for sounding so calm and reasonable. "Just talk to me, *please*."

Grrr.

She hated it when he did that.

Made her feel like a child holding a grudge.

"Fine," she snapped, pulling her attention from the hummingbird to glare at him, refusing to be moved by the look of sheer relief on his face. "Glory needs the Guard more than we do. No one's seen her since the Veils fell and I'm worried about her."

"I know you are, Astra, but your sister can take care of herself. Her magic is a lot more offensive than yours. Besides, according to that interweb thing, she had many more Guardians at her side than we did here. The majority of *our* forces were delayed by the Sorenalaya and trapped inside Faerie, whereas Guardians literally *poured* through the Eastern Veil to protect Glory. With that many Guardians at her side, I'm sure she's fine."

"Then why haven't we heard from her? Why has no one seen her since the cameras went dark? Why did the mortal government shut down all communications from D.C.?"

Kahji sighed. "I have no idea."

"Well, I do. She's in trouble. I can feel it. While the mortals here have more or less accepted our presence—"

Kahji let out a snort of derision.

"Okay, fine, but progress is definitely—possibly, kind of—being made. At least I know we're safe behind our shield, whereas we have no idea what is happening in D.C. because they're not communicating. No news has come out of that city in four weeks and the last sight I had of my sister was of her being surrounded by entire troops of well-armed, hostile mortals. Obviously, she needed the Guard more than I did, but I still kept half of them, didn't I?"

"You did and I appreciate it, but Astra, you can't be naive. These mortals aren't our friends. They want this land back and they want us gone."

"Well, they can't have it back, now can they? I believe I've made that quite clear."

In fact, Astra had lost her temper on a couple memorable occasions as the police officers she'd ejected that first day in the mortal realm were replaced by something called the National Guard and then by increasing numbers of mortals who only ever identified themselves with initials—the FBI, the CIA and the NSA, to name a few.

Each confrontation, she'd claimed more land for the

Fae, ejecting the interlopers with the same vast display of power as before.

"You *have* made it clear. However, I'm finding it difficult to reconcile your behavior with the fact that you're supposed to be our *diplomatic* Princess," Kahji said dryly.

Astra whirled and glared at him. "What did you expect me to do?"

"I don't know. Enter into diplomatic conversations. Negotiate with the mortals."

"*Negotiate?* They opened fire and you were bleeding immortal blood everywhere, Kahji. You and Mitaru and seven others were down in seconds. If the magic of Faerie hadn't returned to us, if my magic wasn't primarily life magic, we would have lost all nine of you, right then. And what do you think would have happened next, Kahji?"

Kahji sighed. "Right. So diplomacy wasn't exactly an option when we were first unveiled, but you haven't even tried since then. It's been four weeks, Astra, and all you've been doing is flexing your power every time the mortals come around."

"Because they don't want to negotiate. They're as arrogant as they ever were and I'm waiting until they approach with a bit of humility, something they have yet to do."

"The problem is with every flex of your power, their determination not to yield just grows."

"Yes, well, *their* problem is every time they force me to flex it, *I get angrier.*"

Astra had never truly understood the phrase "blinding rage" until that terrible moment when she'd first seen Kahji lying so still on the ground, blood spreading beneath him, eyes closed, moments from death. In that moment, every mortal in the vicinity, possibly even the world, had been in terrible danger, for she had wanted them all to *burn.*

Now, every time the mortals demanded she return their lands, she flashed back to that moment—to how still he'd been, to the knowledge of how close she'd come to losing him and worse, to losing him without truly understanding the depths of that loss—and it took everything in her to restrain the darker side of her magic, a darker side she would have sworn didn't even exist six weeks ago.

Rather than give into that darkness each time, Astra instead calmly reminded the mortals that the Fae had taken the lands in payment for the blood the mortals had shed, and then she claimed yet more lands, because *obviously* they hadn't yet learned their lesson.

"Did you really have to surround the entire city with your forest?" Kahji demanded.

Astra shrugged. "I asked the magic where it wanted

to go. It was as impatient as me. Clearly grabbing a couple acres at a time wasn't making enough of an impression. The magic wanted what it wanted."

"And you had nothing to do with it."

Truthfully, Astra had lost patience with the mortals, but she wasn't going to admit that. "Well, I suppose I did, but you know how my magic is. It's *life* magic, completely intertwined with the magic of Faerie, and it's not easy to control. It wants what it wants and ever since we arrived here, all that it wants is to heal this land. *All* of these lands. It's hard to reign in, especially when I know that yielding back these lands would be reinstating their death sentence."

Kahji didn't speak for a moment. When he did, his voice was quiet. "Sometimes late at night, I can hear them screaming."

"I hear them all the time, Kahji, and I now believe with everything in me that *this* is why we Fae were called here. Like it or not, the lands of Faerie *are* connected to the lands of this earth, and if *they* die, it will not be long before Faerie follows."

Kahji nodded. "You're right. I just have to wonder. How did we not realize things had deteriorated to this extent?"

"Because we're as bad as the mortals, Kahji. We only care about our own interests and we've had no real interests on the mortal side of the Veils for millennia.

We may travel here occasionally, but no Fae has stayed long enough to realize how interconnected our lands really are, and now we're all paying the price for our stupidity and selfishness.

"So yes. Building the forest *was* necessary. It was a message to the mortals, but it was also a critical first step in protecting Faerie."

Because the healthier the mortal lands surrounding the doorways were, the healthier the lands of Faerie would be. In a way, the mortals' refusal to accept their new reality was a boon for Faerie because it gave Astra an excuse to continually push the boundaries of the lands they had claimed.

This latest confrontation, though, had ended Astra's patience with the mortals and the games they played.

She was done with making her point through tiny incremental, boundary shifts, and instead, had sent her magic rippling underground throughout the entire city of Lawrence.

Giant slabs of concrete and asphalt had cracked beneath the spreading roots of her magic. Flowers and trees had bloomed everywhere.

Vines had sprouted from the ground, overtaking houses and buildings, lampposts and electrical towers.

Lights had flickered all over Lawrence and the interweb, as Kahji called it, had died, and for a moment, the entire city had gone dark. But then the magic of

Faerie had absorbed the intent of the technological grid of Lawrence and everything had come back.

The Fae now not only had access to the mortal web, but they had their own Fae web as well, and their access was not confined to tiny devices like it was for the mortals.

The Fae could now access the web on any flat surface with just a tiny bit of concentration and magic.

They had succeeded in connecting with the Guardians of the Northern Veil just the day before and had connected to those of the Southern Veil the day before that.

It was their inability, though, to connect with those of the Eastern Veil that had led Astra to send half her Guardians to find and protect Glory.

"I still don't like it," Kahji said.

Astra knew he wasn't speaking of the forest or protecting faerie. Instead, without any warning or change in subject, he had returned them to the conversation about the Guardians of the Veil, making Astra realize how often he did that. Despite never acknowledging their bond, he constantly accessed it, even if only to subconsciously align their conversations with her thoughts.

"We don't have enough Guardians here in Lawrence to truly hold these lands, not if the mortals decide to wage war."

"We have plenty of Guardians for that, Kahji."

"We do not. Did you see how many mortals were in the stands? We are outnumbered, literally thousands to one."

"Which is why I built the forest and created a secondary shield."

When Astra's magic had reached the edges of Lawrence, leaving all of the lands of Lawrence blanketed in its power, she'd built the forest around the perimeter, then another shield to encompass everything, effectively cutting Lawrence off from the rest of the world.

"In another week or so, I'll create a pathway through the woods."

"Just one?" Kahji asked dryly.

Astra sighed. "Fine. Two. I'll make a path on the eastern side and another on the western side, but just because I'm going to give the mortals a couple points of entry and exit doesn't mean the woods will let them in."

"What in all the fates does that mean?" Kahji demanded.

"Look, it's not my fault the magic of Faerie has its own ideas about how to heal these lands. It's changing them and there's nothing we can do about it. Even if I create paths through the woods, there's no guarantee the trees will allow the mortals through. If the trees judge them unworthy, they will simply become lost and the forest will spit them back out on the mortal side of the woods once more."

Kahji just stared at her. "You grew a Judicia Forest here, on the mortal side of the Veils?"

Astra hesitated. "I'm not sure *grew* is the right word. I think the forests of Faerie sent their roots here. The forest was already waiting underground when my magic reached the edges of Lawrence. At that point, the trees just *exploded* into being."

"That shouldn't even be possible."

"And yet, that's what happened."

"Are you even in control of your magic, Astra?"

"As much as I ever am. I've told you before—*it wants what it wants.*"

Kahji groaned. "So basically, the answer is no. You're *not* in control."

Astra rolled her eyes.

She had no idea why Kahji was so obsessed with control.

It was always, "A princess must maintain control at all times," and never, "Losing control can be wonderfully fun in the right circumstances."

"This is not what we need to be worrying about right now, Kahji. It's time for us to step out into the mortal world and make our presence known."

"I think we've managed that quite well enough already, and in fact, have made any number of enemies as a result. We need to stay here, safely behind the shield, until the Veils open again and we can go home."

Astra shook her head. "That isn't going to happen, Kahji, not anytime soon. We're here for a reason and until that reason is met, the Veils won't let us back into Faerie."

"And how do you know that?"

"I just do. We have to actually participate in our destinies if we're going to meet them."

"You can meet your destiny just fine right here behind the shield of Faerie."

"Or not. Kahji, come on. It's time to step out of this bubble we're living in."

Kahji raised an eyebrow, then turned and stared at the castle behind them. "Some bubble."

"We needed shelter and I'm quite aware of the mortals' stories of the Fae. Little flying things who live in fairy tale castles. Well, we can't fly and we don't have wings and we're certainly not the size of insects, but I could give them a castle, so I did."

Astra had never used her magic to build something so elaborate before. She had needed not just life magic, but an incredible amount of earth magic as well. It had been exhausting and fun, first coaxing the land to rise into a hillside that could become home to the Fae, then tunneling it out and shaping it into elaborate rooms built into the landscape.

All of the Guardians had helped and the end result was truly magnificent: a castle made entirely of the living earth.

The roof was made of vines that shielded the structure in inclement weather and retreated when the weather was nice.

The furnishings were made of living trees that adjusted and moved according to the needs of the Fae at any given time.

The entire site had become a bit of a tourist attraction for some mortals and a place to protest for others. Of course, they had to do all their admiring and protesting from outside the primary shield Astra had constructed.

"I don't think a castle, no matter how pretty, is going to make up for destroying the mortals' stadium. They're still quite angry about it, Astra, and it's not like you built the castle for them. It's *our* castle. All *they* can do is look at it from afar and stew over the fact that it isn't their precious football stadium."

Astra let out a huff of exasperation. "I have no idea why these mortals are so obsessed with a game. You would think they would be grateful. After all, we're saving their land, healing it for generations to come."

"Yeah, I don't think they care about that, at least not as much as they care about football."

"Foolish mortals."

"Astra, there's a mortal at the edge of the shield, demanding to speak with you." Toren, one of Kalina's unit left behind, poked his head in to say.

"What does the mortal want?"

"He refuses to say."

Astra rolled her eyes. "Fine. Let's go see what new and interesting thing the mortals have to share today."

"Now, Astra, let's not do anything rash." Kahji hurried to catch up with her. "We need a new strategy since you've pretty much claimed the entirety of Lawrence at this point."

"Princess Astra!"

A man stood just outside the primary shield.

Of course, that meant he was *inside* the secondary one.

That was definitely going to be a problem.

The trees surrounding Lawrence would certainly refuse entry to any mortals they judged unworthy, but they could do nothing about the worthless ones already *inside* the shield.

The mortal waved an arm at her, papers fluttering in his hand.

"You've been served!" He shouted, then flung his hand wide.

The papers he'd been clutching flew across the field, then fell to the ground.

Astra rolled her eyes. "Am I supposed to know what that means?"

"I think you're supposed to collect the papers," Kahji said, "though I'm not sure why you'd want to."

When none of the Fae moved, the mortal shrugged his shoulders, turned and walked away.

"Do you want me collect them?" Toren asked. "Just in case?"

Astra grinned. "Absolutely. If nothing else, they should prove quite entertaining."

CHAPTER 4

"Y ou're not going," Kahji said.

"You heard Zanzor." They had consulted with him when they'd realized the papers they'd gathered were legal documents. Not that Zanzor was an expert in mortal legal matters, but he did know more about the mortal realm than most of them, having spent every vacation there for hundreds of years. "It's a summons to court."

"What do we care about mortal courts? We're the Fae. We do not bow to mortal demands. You're *not* going."

Astra dragged in a deep breath and struggled for patience. "But this is a perfect way to gain a broader audience."

"What are you talking about? We don't need an

audience, let alone a broader one."

"Of course, we do. We need the mortals not associated with the government to want us here. We need the mortal residents of Lawrence to want us here."

"Yeah, that's not going to happen. We've *destroyed* their town. Their ridiculous stadium is gone. We took over a large portion of their college campus and half the students fled the area. Fae magic has wreaked havoc on the foundations of their homes and many are in danger of losing their jobs now that you've enclosed the city and they can't get to work."

Astra waved a hand. "Minor details."

"Minor—Astra! Listen to yourself. I know you're a Fae princess, but you can't possibly be that oblivious to the hardships we're causing the mortals here."

Astra groaned.

"You should just tell him, Astra," Andri said.

Kahji's eyes narrowed. "Tell me what? You're a member of the Royal Guard, Andri. And I'm the Captain of that Guard. If you know something, you need to speak up now."

Andri just shook her head. "I'm sorry, sir, but Astra outranks you. She is a princess and I cannot share what she has forbidden."

"Stop glaring at her," Astra snapped. "It's not her fault. We've been helping in the city the last two weeks."

"Helping how?"

"Providing food, fixing crumbling foundations, building a new stadium."

"Building a new—what?"

Astra shrugged. "I figured it would go a long way toward appeasing the mortals, you know, if we built them a new stadium. It's much better than the original. We created it from mostly organic materials and it's quite large. They should be thrilled."

"Should be? Are you telling me you're building a massive structure somewhere in Lawrence without the approval of city officials?"

"How did that even go unnoticed?" Zanzor asked.

"Magic," Astra and Andri chorused.

"Who else have you roped into this and how have I not noticed you've been leaving the shielded areas?" Kahji demanded.

Astra shrugged. "Most of the Guardians of the Veil have been happy to help. It's been rather boring around here since we finished building the stables and the gardens and the castle and well, everything else. The only thing interesting that happens anymore is when the alphabet soup mortals show up."

"Alphabet soup?" Zanzor asked.

"A mortal phrase. I quite like it. Anyway, I'm certain showing up in court in—what was it again? Two weeks' time—will liven things up."

"You're not going and that's final."

Two weeks later

It was madness at the courthouse. Somehow word had spread that the Fae would be in court that day and there were cameras, tourists, journalists, protestors and more all gathered outside.

Two would-be assassins were delivered Fae justice within five minutes of Astra and her Guard arriving on the court steps. A third and fourth assassin were dealt within *inside* the courthouse.

These humans aren't very smart, are they? a haughty voice demanded from below.

Astra glanced down and smiled. "Well, look at you." She crouched down and stroked a hand down the back of the small animal sitting there. "You're so soft. I've never had the opportunity to meet a mortal four-legged being before."

The animal placed her two front paws on Astra's knee and said, *You can pick me up if you like.*

"Why, thank you." Astra swept the animal into her arms and stood, cuddling her against her chest. "What are you doing here anyway?"

Came to see what all the fuss was about, that's all.

"Hey! No cats allowed." A burly security guard barreled toward them. "Put it outside."

Kahji stepped in front of Astra and rested his hand on the hilt of his sword, the same sword he'd already drawn on several humans that morning. "Step away from the Princess."

The guard skidded to a halt, blinked, then blustered, "Look. No animals are allowed inside the courthouse. It's a rule."

"Well, I don't see any purpose to that rule," Astra said. "We'll be breaking it. Come along now." She turned and strode down the hallway.

Her Guard all scrambled to keep up.

Alarms went off as they walked through devices Astra recognized as metal detectors and she smirked a little as the mortal guards scrambled after them, yipping, "No weapons allowed in the courthouse!"

"Do you know where we're going, Astra?" Kahji demanded as he scared the security guards off with a lethal look.

"Not a clue!" Astra said cheerfully. "Let's explore, shall we?"

Kahji groaned as the rest of the Guard chuckled.

It really was the best morning ever.

Astra got to pop her head into courtrooms and see live court in action.

Of course, the mortals weren't too thrilled when she flung open doors and interrupted their proceedings, but Astra found it all utterly fascinating.

Eventually, a couple mortals gathered the courage to approach and instruct them on where to go and they arrived at the correct courtroom.

Astra wasn't as amused once they were inside.

The mortals *still* hadn't learned that their laws did not apply to the Fae.

They tried to show land documents proving they owned the lands where the Fae had now settled—as if the Fae cared what some mortal documents said.

Astra took great delight in educating the mortals, including sharing the fact that land was a living entity that supported all life living upon it, and as such, could not be *owned*. "It would be like you mortals treating your mother or father as a possession," she explained. "They support you, nourish you and you repay them by claiming ownership of them? That's not right. The land *belongs* to no one, but it is mother and father to *everyone*. In fact, it is parent to this cat as much as it is parent to you or me."

The mortals, of course, had many arguments, but it was the woman the others called Your Honor who summarized it all as, "Opinion is not fact, nor is it a legal defense."

Whatever that meant.

Astra heaved a giant sigh. "Fine then. To speak only facts, in our legal defense, the Fae *do* have the right to lay claim to the entirety of the land the university lies upon."

"Excuse me?" The judge looked stunned.

"In fact, the Fae were the original inhabitants of all the land masses of this world. That we retreated from the earth four millennia ago does not change anything."

"If you have no proof—" Your Honor said.

"Proof that four thousand years ago, we Fae owned this land? Since ownership of land is not something we Fae believe in, we do not."

"Well, then—"

"However, we do not require proof."

"Excuse me?"

"We came here today for two reasons and neither is to provide proof to a mortal court we do not answer to. Instead, we are here out of both courtesy and curiosity. It should concern you, though, to know that we are no longer curious, for when the Fae have no curiosity, impatience seeps in, and with impatience comes intolerance, and with intolerance, often, death."

"Are you seriously standing here in *my* courtroom, threatening me?" Your Honor demanded.

"Not at all. I am standing here in a courtroom that exists on top of *Fae* land, and I am making you, and all mortals, a promise. Do *not* make me keep that promise."

Dead silence.

"Let me repeat what is clearly a difficult concept for

you mortals to grasp: *all land in this world was originally inhabited by the immortal Fae.* As such, it has been, currently is and always will be under our protection. Let me repeat that: this land is under *our* protection and we *will* defend it against *any* who would harm it. It is to your great advantage that we have only reclaimed a tiny percentage of the land we protect.

"When we yielded this land to mortals four millennia ago, we did so to the indigenous peoples of this world. The descendants of *those* peoples are the only ones who *may* have equal rights to the lands of this world, and by equal rights, I mean the right to protect the lands, not own them. Unfortunately, since approximately ninety percent of those indigenous peoples were eradicated as part of your nation's historical legacy, this means *very few* mortals have *any* rights to these lands.

"Having said all of that, we are *not* forcing any mortals to leave this city. They may remain and enjoy all the benefits that come from living in a city now controlled by the Fae. We can be quite generous. I hope many will choose to stay and enjoy our hospitality. Good day."

With that, Astra scooped up the cat currently sprawled across the table in front of her and swept from the courtroom, her Guard falling in step behind her.

About time, the cat muttered.

CHAPTER 5

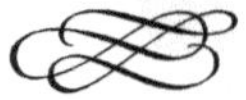

$\mathcal{E}$very time Kahji witnessed Astra in full-on Princess of the Universe mode, he got hard.

He found her sexy when she was just breathing, let alone when she brought out the attitude.

The minute she started speaking in that superior, implacable tone—the one that said she'd as soon set the mortals on fire as speak with them—he could barely breathe through the heat that poured through him.

By the fates, he'd been both blessed and cursed to have such a mate.

Though she had finally started speaking to him again after three days of pure torture, things were not good between them.

Anytime he tried to approach the subject of their mating, she simply stood and walked out. He'd finally come to realize how deeply he'd hurt her and how much damage he had done to their matebond.

He couldn't even explain why he'd made that decision so long ago.

It seemed as if he'd waited forever to make her his and he'd looked forward to her hundredth birthday the way a Sorenalaya craved the souls of mortals.

However, the closer that day had come, the more he'd realized she needed more time. More time to grow into her power and into her independence. He could not take from her the destiny she'd been born to, the Fae she would righteously become if allowed to fully mature on her own.

And so he'd done the hardest thing he could ever imagine.

He'd given her another hundred years.

Surely, that would be enough time so that when he did claim her, she would not become lost in *them*, but would remain the strong Princess Astra he knew she would one day become.

And so another hundred years had passed, a thing of torture unlike anything he'd ever experienced. The closer they came to the end of that second century, the lighter he'd felt. He was certain he'd made the right decision and knew that Astra would forgive him for making her wait another hundred years.

Then, something had happened that last year and

his thinking had gotten all twisted again. He'd been sure, absolutely positive, that she still wasn't ready and releasing the pathway was the wrong decision, so he'd held off again.

For another hundred years, he'd thought, but then that birthday came and went and still he never released the path.

As time passed, he became more convinced, rather than less, that it was the right thing to do because he was not the right one for her. It also became easier to hold the pathway closed, to the point that it became instinct and habit rather than conscious thought.

Now, trapped in the mortal realm, far from the Palace of Faerie, he was seeing those eleven hundred years with far greater clarity than ever before, and was wondering how he could have ever thought giving up his mate was the right thing to do. In fact, the more time that passed, the more convinced he became that something was not right about the way he'd continually avoided the bond.

Every hundred years, on the anniversary of Astra's birth, he'd planned to tell her, to release the path, yet every time, he'd chosen not to, and he simply could not understand why.

Of course, he was unworthy of her.

Any Fae would be as Astra was extraordinary, and *no* Fae warrior was worthy of a matebond.

They *all* had blood on their hands while a matebond was a thing of beauty and purity and light.

That was still no reason to deny it, though, especially when it meant dooming Astra to the silence of a life without it.

He had done that to her. *He* had denied her centuries of bonding with her mate, of feeling complete and whole and cherished.

Realizing exactly what he had done, he had no idea how to approach her now, what to say.

He couldn't tell her what he suspected. It didn't make any sense and besides, he couldn't prove any of it, given they were locked out of Faerie.

Worse, it would look like he was trying to pass the responsibility to someone else when the only one to blame for their lack of a matebond was him.

"Are you really going to bring the cat with us?" Dyranel asked.

"Don't be ridiculous," Kahji said at the same time that Astra said, "Of course, I am."

"What?" Kahji exclaimed. "But it's a mortal cat."

"What's your point?"

Kahji had many points, the first being that mortal cats did not belong with Fae creatures who lived for tens of thousands of years. It was never a good idea for a Fae to become attached to any creature whose life-span was so different from their own.

Unfortunately, he could tell by the look on Astra's face that nothing he said would convince her to leave the cat behind, and might in fact, anger her further, a possibility that made him shudder.

"I was just surprised," he said. "Do you want me to hold her while you mount your—" He broke off as Astra leapt onto her steed, the cat still cradled in her arms. "Never mind then." He swung up on his own horse and with Astra at his side, rode back toward their territory. Or more accurately, *through* their territory toward their more secured territory.

At this point, he imagined it was all pretty secure, especially now that the magic of Faerie had sought out and pulverized all non-Fae weapons within the city, a fact he'd discovered when the first would-be assassin attacked with something the mortals called a baseball bat. Apparently, it was something used in one of their weird battle-games and wasn't considered a weapon at all.

Astra had muttered her new mortal word of the day, "Bullshit," when she'd heard that one.

Kahji grinned at the memory.

"What's so funny?" Astra asked.

It was the first time she'd initiated a conversation in weeks.

"Just remembering the fun we had disarming the mortal assassins."

Astra rolled her eyes. "Like they were a challenge at all."

"You never know. That sculpture looked sharp. It could have done some damage."

"Right."

Kahji chuckled. "So what's up with the cat?"

"Her name's Safira."

"You've already named it?"

"What? Of course not. I would never change someone's name. That would be rude. She told me her name."

"The mortal cat told you its name," Kahji repeated. She couldn't be serious.

"She did, yes."

"You do know that mortal cats cannot speak."

"How would you know?"

"Because it may have been a while since I've traveled to the mortal realm, but I *do* remember that none of the mortal animals were ever capable of speaking."

"Maybe they just didn't like you."

Kahji let out a growl of frustration. "I'm serious, Astra. Mortal cats cannot communicate."

He's not very smart, is he?

Kahji almost fell off his horse, he was so surprised. "Did the cat just talk?" He demanded suspiciously.

"Of course, she did."

"How long have cats been able to talk in this realm?"

"How would I know? Probably forever."

Yes, the cat agreed. *Forever. But only recently have humans been able to understand us.*

"Recently?" Kahji repeated. "As in the current generation has evolved the ability to understand animals?"

No. Recently as in the last couple of weeks. None of the humans could understand me, and then, suddenly, some of them could.

Though you're the first ones who have responded.

All the others have just stared wide-eyed, then exclaimed they were going mad and ran away. Though a few called me demon cat first.

"I'm speechless," Kahji said.

"Well, that's a first," Astra said.

"Not really. I have no idea what to say to you to make things right, how to apologize, how to explain."

"Then don't."

Oooh. What did he do? Safira peered around Astra's shoulder at Kahji.

Suddenly realizing that Astra couldn't just walk out of the room—though she might decide to ride away—Kahji decided to plead his case, even though it meant the other Guardians might hear him grovel.

"He broke my heart," Astra said to the cat.

I don't think that's something he can make right. Is it?

"No. It is not."

Nevertheless. "Astra, I have adored you from the moment I met you."

"Please don't."

"If you think I kept this from you because I don't want you, nothing could be further from the truth."

"Kahji, please."

Kahji guided his horse in front of hers, then circled around as her mount came to a stop. He angled close and cradled her face in his hands, lifting her chin and catching her gaze with his.

The rest of the Guard circled around them, facing outward, providing a shield from the many mortals gathered around, watching as they progressed down what was left of Eleventh Street.

"You have always been the reason for every breath in my body, the life in my limbs, the hope in my heart."

"Kahji."

"I will spend the rest of my days regretting my idiocy and striving to show you how very much I adore you. If you choose never to accept me as your mate, I will understand, but I will never stop trying to prove my love for you."

*A*stra's breath hitched in her throat as she stared into Kahji's eyes.

She wanted to believe him, but a part of her was still terrified he would change his mind.

"You spent eleven hundred years walking away, Kahji. Why should I believe you want me now?"

"I have always wanted you, Astra. Always. I cannot explain what happened or why I became so convinced that I was not the right mate for you, but I am here now and I promise, on my honor, that I will never walk away again."

"If you feel this way, then why is our pathway still closed?"

"That is not a step I will take without your permission, Astra. I held it closed, without consulting you, for over a thousand years. I will not open it again without your consent."

The need for him was an ache inside her heart, a yearning from the depths of her being, to hear his voice inside her head, to feel the forging of their path.

She could not deny either one of them the mate-bond they had both yearned a thousand years for.

"Open the path, Kahji."

He stared into her eyes for a moment, searching for something, perhaps proof of her sincerity. "Very well, my love."

Something deep inside pulled tight, then released with a snap.

Astra?

Kahji.

"Kahji, Princess Astra, I am sorry to interrupt," Rashideh said, "but the mortals are becoming entirely too bold. We need to keep moving."

Astra giggled. "Yes. This is not the right time or place." *Come, Kahji. Let us go home. Well, to our temporary home, anyway. We have a mating ceremony and celebration to plan.*

The incandescent joy on Kahji's face stole all the breath from Astra's lungs.

They rode the rest of the way in silence, but it was not an empty one. It was filled with things unsaid, the pathway connecting the two of them vibrating with love and joy, and the feel of their matebond waiting, poised on the precipice of destiny.

CHAPTER 6

"The mortals are following us," Zanzor reported a few moments later.

"Interesting, isn't it?" Astra said. "The magic of Faerie is transforming everything. The lands, the animals, even the people."

"What are you talking about?" Kahji asked.

"The mortals must have sensed that something momentous is about to happen and that's why they're following us."

"Or maybe they're just interested in the Fae."

Astra grinned. "Perhaps. Either way, we should let them attend our matebond ceremony. They can serve as witnesses to the joy of a Fae mating. Perhaps it will soften their hearts toward us."

"I wouldn't count on it," Kahji said, "and they can be witnesses from behind the shield."

"Then let's have our ceremony near the lake. It's close enough to the shield, they'll be able to get a good view."

"Whatever you want, my love."

Two hours later, Astra stood facing Kahji, next to the lake she had claimed in a territory expansion several weeks before, with her heart in her throat.

The Guardians were all there as witnesses, as were a large number of mortals on the other side of the shield.

Even Safira was there, standing on a bench, watching.

"Astra." Kahji drew in a deep breath, then spoke the traditional vows solemnly. "I see eternity in your eyes and no matter the length of our days, I shall know peace so long as you are by my side. I offer you everything that I am, everything that I have been and everything I've yet to become, in this realm and in any other, in this lifetime and in all the rest."

Astra smiled, for that bit about realms was his own addition.

"With you, *for* you, Astra, I am my best self."

The joy Astra felt, listening to Kahji speak vows she'd begun to believe she would never hear, was incandescent, as was the joy she felt in speaking those same vows back to *him*, the one Fae she had loved from the beginning and would love through all the remaining days of her life.

"Kahji. I see eternity in your eyes and no matter the length of our days, I shall know peace so long as you are by my side. I offer you everything that I am, everything that I have been and everything I've yet to become, in this realm and in any other, in this lifetime and in all the rest."

Kahji grinned at her and she finished her vows with a smile on her face. "With you, *for* you, I am my best self."

A thousand blessings be upon this mating. It was the cat, Safira, who spoke the traditional Fae blessing, but it was Queen Naira's voice and Queen Naira's magic that rained down upon Astra and Kahji in tiny little bursts of power, a royal blessing from the Fae side of the Veil, bringing their matebond to throbbing life.

*B*efore Kahji had a chance to even think of kissing his mate, the other Guardians had leapt forward and separated the two.

In Faerie, the Fae would travel for days to attend a Fae mating celebration, for they were traditionally full of laughter, music and dancing, and were an opportunity to celebrate the joining of two Fae souls.

Though no Fae traveled to attend Kahji's mating celebration with Astra, and though the number of Fae in attendance was possibly the lowest number in the history of the Fae—six Royal Guardians and thirteen Guardians of the Veil—the celebration was still as joyful and as full of tradition as Kahji could have hoped for.

The Fae Guardians outdid themselves.

They used earth magic to coax the land into providing a dance floor and the trees and wind into providing music.

They whirled Astra and Kahji onto the dance floor and worked hard to keep the two close enough to yearn for each other, but not close enough to actually touch.

The mortals on the other side of the shield leapt into their own preparations. They set up their own dance floor, brought out musical instruments and joined the celebration.

The mortal crowd grew as word spread that a Fae celebration was happening.

Children arrived and ran around, laughing and dancing, and though there was a shield between Fae and mortal, it felt like one big celebration.

"You were right," Kahji called to Astra as several

Guardians whirled her past where he was dancing with Dyranel and Zanzor.

"About what?" she called to him over Talveney's shoulder.

Kahji had to wait to answer because Dyranel pulled him into an intricate dance step that required all his concentration and when he looked up, Astra had disappeared behind a wall of Guardians.

It was a while before Kahji saw her again. This time, she was in Rashideh's arms. "About inviting the mortals. It feels like a true mating celebration."

"That's because it is one!" Rashideh exclaimed as he whirled Astra into Kahji's arms.

Not one to miss an opportunity like that, Kahji immediately pulled Astra close and kissed her.

*A*stra had waited over a thousand years for this one kiss, but as heat rolled through her, she knew she would have waited ten thousand more.

She lifted high onto her toes, wrapped her arms around Kahji's shoulders and strained closer, pouring everything she had into that kiss.

Breathing him in—*her mate, her fated one, her life*—Astra lost all sense of time and place.

"I do believe that's quite enough of that." Toren pulled her from Kahji and though she strained to get back to him, the Guardians formed a wall between her and Kahji again, and Toren whirled her into Lumina's arms.

She giggled as Lumina swept her around in a circle, then sent her spinning into Andri's arms, who spun her into Korel's.

In this way, the Guardians kept her and Kahji dancing far from each other most of the night, though every once in a while, they conspired for them to meet on the dance floor.

Sometimes, it was barely long enough for them to touch a hand. Other times, they had just enough time for a flaming hot kiss before they were separated again.

As the hours passed, the heat between them built until Astra could barely breathe for wanting her mate, especially since Kahji kept talking to her through their bond, murmuring delicious things to her, even as they were kept apart.

Though they were now mated, their matebond secure, he was still courting her, wooing her, seducing her with his voice.

I cannot wait to taste you again, my sweet Astra.

I've waited centuries for our mating, and tonight, when we lie skin to skin, I will remember those many lonely years and take my time making you mine.

Astra, my love, you are a fire in my blood and I burn for you.

Every moment we are together for the rest of our lives will be a blessing I will never take for granted.

I look forward to peeling that gown from your body and learning every contour of it with my hands and my tongue.

Ah, my love, my Fae princess, my Astra, I wonder how you will taste.

Sweet and exquisitely fine, no doubt.

It was only as the skies around them lightened, heralding the approaching dawn, that Astra and Kahji were finally allowed to escape to have their own, more private celebration.

By that time, Astra was as close to spontaneously combusting as she imagined any Fae had ever been.

Holding hands, she and Kahji ran around the pond and headed for the castle, the cat, Safira, who had joined in the dancing, at times weaving between dancers' feet and at others cradled in Fae arms, darting behind them.

Kahji led Astra through the front entrance of the castle and veered them immediately to the left.

Astra had expected him to take her up the back stairs to where the bedrooms were.

Instead, he let her toward the western tower.

Astra, Lumina and Andri had spent hours pouring over images of mortal castles, particularly the towers, and had used air and earth magic to perfect their versions of them.

They had tunneled out a ramp inside the towers that wound round and round to the roof. The earth and vines closed off the top of the ramp in poor weather, but otherwise, it led right out onto the roof of the tower.

They had also created a walkway that ran across the front wall of the castle, connecting the two towers.

Astra found the shape of the battlements at the top of the walls of the towers and the walkway to be charming and preferred not to think of how mortals had used them to wage war.

Though it had taken quite some time to create the towers and walkway, they really were just decorative in nature. The Guardians sometimes used them to see far into the distance, to judge where mortals were in relation to the shield that surrounded them, but otherwise, they weren't exactly the heart of the castle.

As such, Astra wondered what Kahji was planning, leading her up the ramp. Perhaps he intended for them to watch the sun rise up there. It would undoubtedly provide an amazing view.

The lighting in the tower changed as the artificial light from the lanterns hung along the walls gave way to the natural light of the dawning day as they reached the end of the ramp and arrived on the roof of the tower.

When she saw what awaited them there, Astra gasped. "How is this possible? We didn't even know we were going to have our ceremony today until just this afternoon."

"The Guardians have been slipping away in groups of two and three to work on this throughout the celebration."

"That's so sweet. It's incredible." The entire area had been transformed into the most beautiful of rooftop gardens. There was a pathway that stretched around the edge of the tower, but the rest of the roof was entirely abloom and at the center of that fragrant, extraordinary garden, a bed created of leaves, flowering vines and juniper branches awaited them.

"The Guardians tell me they learned their lesson when building Kalina and Thorne's bed, which is why they didn't try to elevate ours." Kahji chuckled.

Astra had no idea why that was so amusing, but she wasn't really interested in hearing the story, at least not at that moment. *What do you say we test out their creation?*

Kahji grinned. *I think that is a splendid idea.*

Race you there! She ran down the path leading to the bed with Kahji just one step behind her.

When she was mere feet from her goal, he hooked an arm around her waist and spun her toward him.

He launched them at the bed, turning so that he hit first and she landed on top of him.

Kahji.

Astra, my love.

They rolled across the bed, kissing and straining to get closer.

Kahji surged back, dragged his tunic over his head, then fell down to kiss Astra once more.

Another few moments of endless, drugging kisses, then he wrestled her gown from her before setting down again to stroke and kiss her and learn what made her burn.

A third time he left her, this time to wrestle with the rest of his clothing.

Astra stripped her undergarments away and lay back to stare at her mate as he kicked off his boots and dragged his trousers free.

She barely had time to admire his gorgeous, muscular form before he was settling back over her, kissing her thoroughly.

Then, there were no more thoughts at all as he clasped her hands in his, stared into her eyes and sank deep.

Kahji. She gasped for breath and lunged upward, burying her face in his neck and wrapping her legs around him.

By the fates, you make me burn. The raspy rumble of his voice made her shudder and a deep fluttering began.

Ah, my love. Kahji settled even more heavily over her, holding himself still, making her writhe in an agony of need.

Kahji, please!

Finally, *finally*, he began to move, pulling out and then surging forward again and again, causing her to cry out as the friction and heat rose to an unbearable degree.

She flung her head back and stared at the skies above them, eyes going blind to the streaks of orange and red setting the world afire as she burned below them in a conflagration of heat, desire and breathless ecstasy.

Kahji's heart pounded as he lay sprawled upon the bed his fellow Guardians had built for him and his princess mate. With Astra sprawled at his side, her head pillowed on his chest, his fingers gently toying with her blue curls, he wondered how the fates had ever deemed him worthy of this incredible gift.

He felt so wonderfully blessed, so fortunate to be

the mate of this singular, extraordinary Fae, he knew he would never be able to express to her how much she truly meant to him and how grateful he was that she had forgiven him his centuries-long mistake.

"Astra, my love," he murmured as she traced her fingers across his Guardian markings.

They had begun as just a few tiny, black leaves stretching up the left side of his neck, but over the centuries had expanded outward, a trailing black vine that stretched across his left shoulder and down his arm, wrapping it in an intricate sleeve of vines.

More recently, the vine on his neck had sprouted new leaves that trailed down the left side of his body, bypassing his groin area to wrap around his thigh.

He often wondered how far the vines would travel, whether they would eventually cross to the right side of his body or if this was as far as they would go.

The markings were part of him, even as they grew and expanded, and he rarely thought about them anymore, other than to note when a new vine sprouted somewhere.

Today, however, he adored them because Astra was slowly stroking her fingers across his chest, tracing the vines' paths down, then up again, spreading heat everywhere she touched.

You know, that's going to get you—oomph. Something landed on his stomach with enough force to expel all his breath and distract him from what he'd been saying. *What the—* he lifted his head, then rolled his eyes at the sight of the cat sitting on his stomach, glaring at him.

Did you really have to bring the cat?

Astra giggled.

The cat's presence was annoying, but it did remind Kahji of something he'd meant to ask. "Did I just imagine Queen Naira's voice blessing our union?"

"I don't think so. After all, my mother is quite powerful. Still, even I was surprised to realize she'd managed to reach through the Veil to bless us on our mating day."

"You'd think she could have found a better candidate for delivering her message than a mortal cat."

Safira hissed and swiped out at him, drawing blood.

"Ow, you little beast!"

"You insulted her. What do you expect?"

"I bet the cat doesn't talk at all. It was probably just your mother messing with us."

Astra lifted up and gave him an incredulous look. "Do you really believe my mother, the Queen of Faerie, used her magic to break through the barrier and reach out to her daughter who is trapped on the mortal side of the realm, just so that she could 'mess with me?'"

"Well, when you put it like that," Kahji grumbled.

I stand by my original observation, Safira said. *The male of the species, any species, just isn't that smart.*

Astra grinned. "We probably shouldn't say that out loud, Safira. At least not where the males can hear us."

Just making sure he understands his place. Beneath me. And you, of course. Well, and every other female on the planet.

Kahji let out a snort of disgust and Astra giggled again.

"I see how this is going to go. Ganged up on by a couple females." Kahji surged upward, causing Safira to launch away with a soft hiss, then turned and bore Astra to the bed, settling heavily over her once more. "I don't mind though." He captured her lips in a searing kiss, murmuring against them as he sank deep, "You can gang up on me anytime you like."

CHAPTER 7

The following days were amazing.

When the sun rose in the sky, the garden around them rose to shield them from the worst of its effects, forming a canopy over their mating bed, then retracted as the sun fell so that they could make love under the stars.

Each morning, they walked across the walkway to the eastern tower where they found a table set up with food and drinks, a new feast provided every morning by the Guardians.

And so the first week of their mating passed, with delicious food and endless lovemaking.

When they finally emerged from the tower, they were greeted with cheers and congratulations.

"Princess Astra, Captain." Dyranel stepped

forward. "Much has happened over the past seven days. Fae have begun arriving in the city of Lawrence from all over the Americas, from wherever they were traveling when the crossings closed. There are encampments as far west as Topeka, as far east as Kansas City, as far south as Wichita and as far north as Omaha.

"The secondary shield around Lawrence is intact. It has not expanded. However, the magic has traveled well beyond our borders and a third shield has gone up around the larger territory."

Astra had to be misunderstanding. "A shield went up without us actively putting it in place? None of you made it happen?"

The Guardians shook their heads.

"What about the other Fae? Could one of them have replicated her shield?" Kahji asked.

"Several of us have been traveling out to make contact with the Fae and to gain an understanding of this third shield," Yiveren, one of the Guardians of the Veil, said. "It truly is a construct of Faerie, made purely of its magic."

"He's right," Toren said. "Astra's shields are a combination of her magic and that of Faerie itself. This third shield has nothing of the Fae, but is everything of Faerie."

"We believe it went up to provide protection to the

Fae who have not made it inside the secondary shield yet," Dyranel said.

"Unfortunately, the mortals are now looking at us as an aggressive and hostile force, here to overthrow their government and destroy their world," Zanzor said. "They have attempted multiple attacks, but the magic of Faerie defends itself quite aggressively. Every mortal weapon within the shield or a hundred miles outside it has been destroyed and no mortal with aggressive intentions has been allowed to cross any of the shields.

"Of course, that hasn't helped with those aggressors already inside them. There have been reports of Fae deaths, though none have gone unpunished. Either the Fae themselves have executed the aggressors or the magic of Faerie has literally incinerated them. This has caused a bit of a panic among the mortals and there was a surge in aggression approximately two days ago."

"You should have come to us immediately," Kahji said with a scowl.

"With all due respect, Captain, there was nothing you could have done," Dyranel said. "None of us can control the magic of Faerie. It wants what it wants."

Astra shivered to hear those words she had often used when describing her own magic.

It wants what it wants.

"The magic of Faerie has made its stance quite clear," Dyranel continued. "It is claiming land for the

Fae who are trapped here and it is defending those Fae quite viciously."

"The interesting thing," Zanzor said, "is that not all the mortals hate what is happening. Many have traveled here to join what they are calling the miracle revolution."

"Miracle revolution? What do they mean by that?" Kahji demanded.

"I believe it refers to the miracle many mortals have hoped for when it comes to the health of their planet," Dyranel said. "They believe this is the revolution needed for the earth to heal itself from all the damage the mortals themselves have caused."

"You should also know that the primary shield isn't holding every mortal out anymore," Zanzor said.

"What do you mean?" Astra exclaimed.

"The mortals are getting inside our primary shield?" Kahji repeated incredulously.

"They are," Zanzor said. "It appears they are all of indigenous blood and they have come to align themselves with the Fae and to express their gratitude and hope for a healthier world."

"All of this happened in just seven days?" Astra exclaimed.

"A video of your mating celebration went viral," Dyranel said.

"What is viral?" Kahji asked.

"A mortal recorded the mating celebration and posted it on a bunch of internet social sites," Dyranel explained. "It was shared over and over again, until it went this thing called viral. It even eventually made its way onto the Fae web. Our brethren saw the mating celebration and they all celebrated with us wherever they were."

"It's really quite amazing," Zanzor said. "We thought your mating celebration was only attended by nineteen Fae, but instead, hundreds celebrated with us throughout the Americas."

"Yes, and when the celebration was over, they started traveling here," Dyranel said, "many of them undertaking an extraordinarily long journey."

"One couple I spoke with came from as far south as Patagonia," Zanzor said.

"How have they been managing it?" Astra asked.

"Horses, mortal transportation such as trains and buses and a whole lot of magic, especially when crossing borders."

The concept of borders was so strange to Astra. To require documents to travel from one place to the next seemed barbaric. All Fae were a community of one, welcome anywhere in Faerie at any time.

Not that they hadn't waged wars throughout their history. It was perhaps the one great tragedy of being such a long-lived race of beings. After so many centuries of living, it could become difficult to find hope in the future, especially if a Fae never found his or her mate.

When that happened, Fae mostly Faded from the world, becoming Sorenalaya, a weaker, more insubstantial version of their most beastly selves. Thin to the point of transparency, armed with claws and fangs, the Sorenalaya craved human flesh and souls and hunted along the borderlands between Faerie and the mortal world, hoping to cross over and feast.

The Guardians were tasked with ending their pain and suffering and sending them into the light. It darkened a Guardian's soul, but also made the Guardians a bright, shining light for all the Fae, for they were the most honorable of them all.

Skirmishes with the Sorenalaya, though, were not wars.

Wars came when something far worse than the Sorenalaya was born of a Fae's darkness, when the Fae who should have Faded remained part of the world instead and were consumed by their darkness, spreading it to those around them.

This was when war happened, when the Fae had to rise up against one of their own and fight the armies of the dark, to bring light back to the world.

There had only ever been one war in Astra's lifetime and she had been a little girl at the time. It had taken six hundred thousand Fae and sixty years to bring that dark Fae down.

Astra hoped never to see the likes of her again.

"My love, are you okay?" Kahji cupped her cheek in concern.

Astra shook away her memories of the dark. "Sorry. Just a ghost walking over my grave."

"What a horrible mortal phrase," Zanzor said, giving an exaggerated shudder.

Horrible, perhaps, but that doesn't make it any less accurate. Safira wound around Astra's legs, rubbing against them. *Do not allow the ghosts of the past to distract you from what is happening right now, Princess Astra.*

"Yes, you're right," Astra murmured. "What should we do?"

Zanzor dragged in a deep breath. "You're not going to like this, Kahji."

Kahji scowled. "What are you thinking?"

"The Fae need to see their Princess, but they also need to see the two of you together. They need to know that there is hope and that the Throne continues to thrive, even here in the mortal realm, so far from home. More, the mortals who would be our allies need to see the two of you together, your strength and your bond. We need to make our own viral video."

Astra giggled. "I don't think we can guarantee a

video will go viral, Zanzor. It simply happens or it doesn't."

He just stared at her.

She rolled her eyes. "Fine. I suppose we could use our glamour and embed some magic in the video and compel them to watch it, but I'm not sure compelling the mortals is a good idea."

Kahji chuckled.

"What?"

"That you believe they will need to be compelled to watch any video starring you, the Fae Princess Astra, is ridiculous, but Zanzor is right. I do not like this plan."

"We're already exposed, Kahji. There is no containing this situation. The only thing we can do is move forward and I absolutely agree that our Fae citizens need to see us and know that we are here for them, that we are working hard to find them a way home. It only makes sense to allow the mortals to see us at the same time. So as a famous mortal captain once said, let's make it so."

*K*ahji hated this plan with a passion, though he wasn't exactly sure why, other than that he wanted to protect his mate and this plan felt reckless.

Astra reassured him multiple times that she could take care of herself, that no mortal could possibly harm her, to which he reminded her that many Fae had already fallen.

They had a list of the Fae taken from them too soon: seventeen names that they knew of, so far, and all of them knew there could be more.

At highest risk were those solitary Fae who had been traveling alone with no warriors to defend them and no glamour to shield them from human eyes during those six long moments when the Veils had fallen and the magic of Faerie had become inaccessible.

The bad news was that none of them knew how many Fae were out there. They had an estimate only.

The Guardians of the Veil monitored all crossings and therefore, believed they had a general idea of how many Fae were typically on the mortal side of the Veils at any given time.

Their best estimate was approximately five thousand.

Still, it was an estimate only and they warned it could be off by a significant amount.

Kahji hated that his mate felt responsible for every single one of those Fae, that she felt compelled to find them and protect them.

All he cared about was protecting her, but the reality was, though she insisted she never wanted the throne of Faerie, to all those Fae currently trapped in the Americas, she *was* the throne.

They looked to her for answers and for hope.

All Kahji could do was stand at her side and support her as she stepped further into her destiny as a Royal Princess of the Fae.

CHAPTER 8

They had been traveling for weeks now, slowly exploring the territories Faerie had claimed for the Fae, interacting with the inhabitants of those territories, both Fae and mortal alike.

Though Astra knew Kahji didn't like it, she appreciated that he never once protested when she hugged Fae who looked lost, when she swept small Fae children up into her arms and entertained them with a bit of Fae magic, or when she held one Fae as she wept for her orphaned children in Faerie while her mate looked helplessly on.

The days were difficult to endure, hearing so many Fae stories of who had been left behind, of why the Fae had come to the mortal realm in the first place—to shop or travel or enjoy a night out with friends—most of the reasons so frivolous, the Fae were leveled by the consequence of such a seemingly innocent decision.

Not worth it, was the cry Astra heard over and over again.

What the Fae had gained in their travels to the mortal realm wasn't worth the terrible sacrifice now being asked of them.

After long days spent with the Fae, Astra and her Guard passed their evenings with the indigenous communities who had traveled from around Kansas and beyond to meet the Fae.

The various tribes shared their traditional stories of how land and lives had been lost in the distant past. Despite the passage of generations and the distance that had been gained from those terrible times, if not from their consequences, the tragedy of it all broke Astra's heart.

That mortals had not cherished each life as part of their community of one, that they had not seen the land as a nourishing parent to be shared by all, that they had instead bathed those lands in blood, steeping them in violence and tears, made her heart tremble.

The nights she spent in Kahji's arms.

He held her as she wept a storm of tears, purging her sorrow and grief from the stories she'd heard that day, then he loved her tenderly through the night hours, setting her body aflame and healing her anew.

Then every morning, they got up to do it all over again.

"The website we set up is getting two million hits a day," Talveney reported at the end of a long day nearly six weeks later.

"I can't keep up with the comments," Andri complained. "I've tried every bit of spellwork I can think of to purge all the racist and hateful comments, but it just doesn't work. Every spell ends up purging some comments it shouldn't and leaving others that it should. It's driving me mad."

Kahji chuckled. He couldn't believe the conversations they were having anymore—the Fae dealing with technology, managing websites and recording videos. It was enough to make him doubt his own sanity. "Well, better you two than me. I do not understand this mortal technology at all."

"It's not so mortal anymore," Talveney said. "At this point, it's really a construct of Faerie."

"Which is why it makes no sense that the spells won't work," Andri said.

"Maybe because if we purge everything we don't want to hear, all we end up with is an echo chamber,"

Astra said. "Perhaps we need to hear what the hateful ones are saying, just so that we can be sure and address the hate, purge it by refuting their words, rather than scrubbing them out entirely."

"Huh." Andri appeared to think about that for a moment. "That might explain why the spells are scooping up the worst of the offenders, the ones there's no point in engaging, like the death threats and things like that, but leaving the opinions of close-minded idiots. Honestly, I don't have to refute them because others—many, many others—take them on beautifully."

"Well, there you have it," Kahji said. "I say, don't waste your time on those idiots. In fact, it'd be nice if we could stop with the recordings as well."

Astra rolled her eyes at him, making him grin.

Even though he understood their purpose, Kahji hated the videos Talveney and Andri had Astra making.

It was why Kahji had insisted on being at her side in every single video and had then made a point of standing, arms crossed, scowling at the camera the entire time.

Astra found it hilarious.

Talveney and Andri just rolled their eyes at him.

As for Kahji, he simply wanted anyone watching to know viscerally that targeting Astra was to risk the most terrible of Fae executions possible.

He would never admit it, but even he could see the

videos were having positive results as they showcased Astra's work traveling through the territories.

Conversations she had with both Fae and mortals were, with permission, recorded and posted on their website, no explanation given, just a title, something like "Meeting with representatives from The Kaw Nation, People of the Southwind" or "Conversations with Fae working to clean the waters of Kansas."

It was the Fae's hope that over time the videos would help the mortals understand the true nature of the lands that supported them and the inherited role and responsibilities that came with being stewards of the land, whether they be Fae or mortal, indigenous or not.

Still, it was the video of a tiny mortal child running up to Astra, arms high for a hug that had garnered the most views.

Astra's beaming smile as she swept the child into her arms, listened to her babble and cuddled her as she napped on Astra's shoulder was the one video that seemed to have charmed an entire nation.

The hostilities from the mortal government had subsided, mostly because it had become clear there would be no displacing the Fae and that they would meet violence of any sort within their territories with swift, Fae justice.

For the most part, the Fae left the mortal courts to

deal with their mortal criminals, but that did not mean the Fae would not strike back should those criminals target the Fae, including when those criminals were government officials.

The Fae also intervened when they became aware of mortals committing crimes against other mortals.

In fact, criminals were delivered with frequent regularity to the police stations closest to where the Fae were staying.

And so the months had passed, with the center of the country known as the United States of America undergoing an extraordinary transformation as more and more Fae arrived and as the land was healed.

Astra assumed a similar transformation was happening on the eastern seaboard, stretching from Washington, D.C. to New York City, but she couldn't be certain because they still had no news from inside that shield.

The shield that had come down around D.C. in the moments following the Fae's arrival had expanded outward to envelop Baltimore, Philadelphia, New York City and all the territories between. It had then frozen there and nothing had happened since.

Fae had initially gathered along that shield's border as well, but when they weren't admitted and no one came out to greet them, they eventually turned toward

Kansas and the Princess whose mating ceremony they had celebrated from afar.

With their arrival came the return of the majority of the Guardian unit Astra had sent east.

"The shield allowed Mitaru through, then Kalina and Thorne, but it refused the rest of us," Jeniah explained. "We wanted to stay and wait, but Kalina directed us to lead the rest of the Fae here, to see if you had new orders for us. The three of them were going to do their best to track Glory down. Mitaru seemed certain they would find her."

That was the last they'd heard from the east.

No other Guardians they sent were able to penetrate the eastern shield and so Lawrence, Kansas, became the mortal home to the Fae Throne, and the territories surrounding it, home to the Fae themselves.

Astra, though she'd had no desire to become queen, found herself serving in that role to the Fae refugees who arrived seeking hope and a bit of Faerie to comfort them in the darkness.

Astra faced that same darkness and it was Kahji who kept her sane, who kept her hope alive, even when she despaired of ever seeing her sister again, of seeing her brothers, of gaining access to their homelands once more.

Each night, when they retired, wherever they were,

Astra turned to Kahji to keep that darkness at bay and this night was no different.

Leaving Talveney and Andri debating what to title the latest video they had just uploaded, Kahji led Astra up the stairs toward their chambers.

When they arrived, he undressed her gently, caressing and dropping a reverent kiss upon each bit of flesh revealed along the way.

Though he took his time with her, he stripped his own clothes with an economy of movement and gently lowered her to their bed, following her down.

My love, he murmured, linking their hands together, palm to palm, staring into her eyes as he sank deep.

Kahji, she whispered, pulling him close, burying her face in his neck and breathing in his familiar, heady scent. *You are my everything.*

As you are mine. Mate. Beloved. Best friend.

Though uncertainty defined their lives, there were no doubts in these moments, no questions, no worries, no insecurities.

They were simply *one.*

Read on for an excerpt from GLORY.

EXCERPT

This was the third Ceremony of the Veil that had occurred in Princess Glory's lifetime, but only the second where she'd been called to serve as royal witness. Even so, she knew two things immediately.

One, the Guardians of the Eastern Veil did not hesitate to perform their sacred duty. They poured their life force over the Veil in a breathtaking act of honor and devotion to the Fae.

And two, their sacrifice was failing.

The fractures in the Veil were not disappearing as they should, but instead were multiplying swiftly.

Before Glory could decide on a course of action, the ground trembled, causing the waters around her to ripple and surge outward, almost as if she were standing in the ocean, rather than a mortal-made pool.

A flash of light exploded from the Veil and everything went dark.

Glory woke surrounded by water.

For a split second, she remembered nothing, then it all came back in a rush.

The Reflecting Pool.

The Eastern Veil.

The mortals on every side.

"Princess Glory." Talvenia, the Captain of her Royal Guard, held out a hand—the one not holding her sword —and pulled Glory to her feet. "The Veil is down."

The rest of the Royal Guard stood around them, swords drawn, facing the mortals who gaped in awe, some of them struggling to their feet, others frozen where they had fallen.

Of all the places in the mortal realm where a doorway to Faerie might have stood, this was not the location Glory would have chosen.

Too many mortals.

Too many cameras.

Too many things that could go wrong.

One only had to look toward Faerie to see that truth.

The doorway that led into their realm was no longer shielded by the Eastern Veil. Instead, the lands and skies of Faerie were completely exposed, providing a glimpse into a world few mortals had ever seen.

Worse, the glamour the Fae had projected to shield themselves from mortal eyes was also down. This was clear from the way the mortals stared even as they recorded everything.

This was a disaster.

At that moment, Fae Guardians poured through the doorway.

As they marched past to stand as a physical, living shield between the mortals and the entrance to Faerie, Glory recognized them as those tasked with strengthening the Eastern Veil.

They would have expected to be nothing but dust on the wind by now, their life force given in tribute to strengthen the Veil.

Instead, they were here, still alive, standing on mortal grounds, the final line of defense for Faerie and all of the Fae.

"We should retreat, Princess Glory," Talvenia said. "Leave the Guardians to protect the entrance to Faerie and—" She broke off as the Veil yanked energy from all of the Fae standing there.

"It's too late," Glory gasped, struggling to breathe through the whiplash sensation of her magic being used to reform the Veil before returning to her in a massive rush of power.

Glory swayed in place, staring at the Veil. It was back, but somehow *wrong*. She reached out with her magic, attempting to get a feel for what she was sensing.

"Why is it transparent?" Xilarin asked. "It should be a doorway, not a window."

"The mortals can still *see* Faerie," Raiyana said, glancing around, a worried look on her face.

"At least it's back up," Talvenia said. "It's stable, right?"

"It's stable." Glory shoved her magic harder at the Veil, testing its strength, probing for a way in. "It's also—"

"What?" Xilarin asked.

"Locked."

"Against *us*?" Raiyana demanded.

"Against everyone, I think." Glory splashed through the water toward the Veil. She reached out and ran her hand over it.

Solid.

Fairly vibrating with magic.

And completely sealed shut.

"How is that even possible?" One of the Guardians of the Veil demanded. Glory thought his name was Nako.

Before she could respond—not that she had an explanation to offer—one of the Fae shouted, "Guardians, defend the Princess. Guard the entrance to Faerie!"

"What's happening?" Glory whirled away from the Veil, but all she could see was her Royal Guard, who surrounded her in force.

Shouts and a strange popping sound filled the air.

Something hit Raiyana, spinning her toward Glory, a fine red mist spraying the air. "Princess—" she gasped as her knees buckled.

Glory lunged forward to catch Raiyana as she fell, but something plowed into Glory with the force of ten thousand Sorenalaya and flung her back.

Time seemed to slow as she fell, pain spreading fire to every nerve in her body.

When she hit the water, droplets sprayed upward in a dance so slow, they almost seemed as if they weren't moving at all.

Glory stared at those droplets, even as she sank below the surface, the fire spreading until it reached the core of who she was and touched the wild magic hiding there.

As the water droplets began their inexorable fall back toward earth, that feral, Fae magic that Glory had spent a millennia containing, exploded from every pore of her being and erased the world in a white wave of power.

Find out what happens next in GLORY.

THE SHENANIGANS SERIES

Shifter Shenanigans

Witchy Shenanigans

Full Moon Shenanigans

Hotel Shenanigans

Dragon Shenanigans

Undercover Shenanigans

Spooky Shenanigans

Holiday Shenanigans

Valentine Shenanigans

Lucky Shenanigans

STORIES OF THE VEIL

Guardians of the Veil

Astra

Glory

Luna

Zara

Lotus

WICKED

No Rest for the Wicked

Wicked Is As Wicked Does

PAWSITIVELY PURRFECT TRILOGIES

THE CAT'S MEOW

Catnapped | The Real McCat | Unbearably Cute

HOLLY JOLLY PAWLIDAY

A Catmas to Remember | This Cat's for You | Santa Kitty

SHENANIGANS ANTHOLOGIES

CRAZED

Books 1-3

AMAZED

Books 4-6

HOLIDAZED

Books 7-10

SHENANIGANS

The Complete Collection

STORIES OF THE VEIL

THE UNVEILED

Astra | Glory

THE VEILED

Luna | Zara

WICKED DUET

WICKED

No Rest for the Wicked | Wicked Is As Wicked Does

ABOUT THE AUTHOR

WWW.PEPPERMCGRAW.COM

Pepper McGraw is a *USA Today* Bestselling Author of paranormal romance. She hasn't met any paranormals to date, but she's sure that moment is just around the corner!

Pepper loves animals, especially cats, and spends her free time volunteering at local shelters and for Trap-Neuter-Release programs.

She's had the supreme honor of winning occasional head butts and meows from the local ferals in her neighborhood and has even convinced a few to come inside and adopt her as their own.

bookbub.com/authors/pepper-mcgraw

facebook.com/ShenanigansSeries

goodreads.com/peppermcgraw

instagram.com/peppermcgraw_author

tiktok.com/@peppermcgraw

twitter.com/peppermcgraw